The Mutiny Bug
A StarSoldier Chronicle
C.R. Coyne

Table of Contents

Also By Me Operation Sabotage:	4
Also By Me World Machine:	5
Map of Human Sphere:	6
Map of Human Sphere #2:	7
History of the Mohawk Tribe:	8
The Mutiny Bug:	10
Chapter II:	14
Chapter III:	16
Chapter IV:	19
Chapter V:	29
Chapter VI:	30
Chapter VII:	34
End:	38
Six Months Later:	50

Feedback:	53
Beta Readers Wanted:	54
My Email:	55
Who I am:	56
Where You Can Find Me:	57
Copyright:	58
Operation Sabotage:	59

Also By CR Coyne

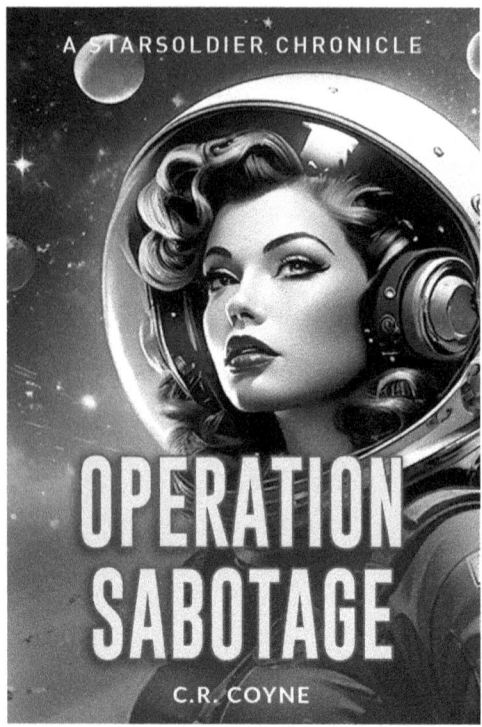

It's just a routine pick up mission. In and out in a few hours no contact with the natives. But the beautiful world of Topaz isn't anymore. Now Yaz and the squad must try and save an entire planet. But if that's not enough first they have to save themselves!

Buy your copy today!

Also By CR Coyne

It's not everyday you crash into a sun and live. But for Yaz and the crew that's not the weird part. In fact that only starts a long list of weird, and problems. After all, it's hard to stay alive when an entire world wants you dead!

Buy your copy today!

Galactic Area of Human Sphere

Star Map of Notable Sites

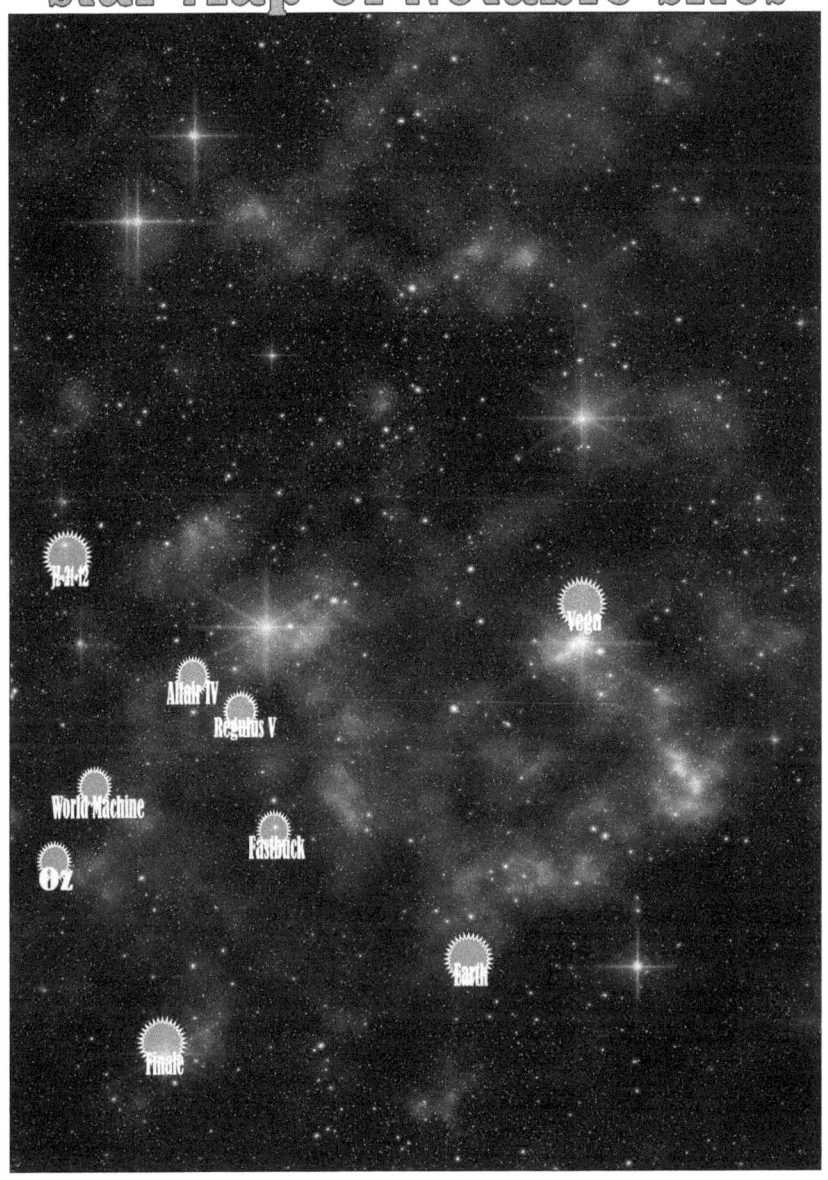

History of the Mohawk Tribe

The Mohawk are traditionally the keepers of the Eastern Door of the Iroquois Confederacy, also known as the Six Nations Confederacy or the Haudenosaunee Confederacy. Our original homeland is the north eastern region of New York State extending into southern Canada and Vermont. Prior to contact with Europeans the Mohawk settlements populated the Mohawk Valley of New York State. Through the centuries Mohawk influence extended far beyond their territory and was felt by the Dutch who settled on the Hudson River and in Manhattan. The Mohawks' location as the Iroquois nation closest to Albany and Montreal, and the fur traders there, gave them considerable influence among the other Tribes. This location has also contributed directly to a long and beautifully complicated history.

In the 1750s, to relieve crowding at Kahnawake and to move closer to the Iroquois homeland, the

French Jesuits established a mission at the present site on the St. Regis River. The Mohawk people had continually used this site at the confluence of the St. Lawrence River Valley as part of our fishing and hunting grounds prior to the building of the first church. "Akwesasne" as it is known today, translates roughly to "Land where the partridge drums" has always been a prime location due to the confluence of several small rivers and the St. Lawrence River.

The Mutiny Bug

A StarSoldier Chronicle

C.R. Coyne

"It's one thing for you to conceptualize the fact the universe wants you dead and quite another when it actually tries it. If you take my meaning." Colonel Hendrix nods quietly and lets me talk so I keep going. "Anyway I think maybe it's time for me to pick up my chips and go find another line of work, I feel like I am running out of lucky cracks."

The colonel frowns at that and shakes her head slightly while asking, "lucky what?"

"Nothing, that's Dutch wearing off on me. The point is I want to resign."

"I don't think the entire universe is out to get you. Isn't that a bit of a overstatement?"

"What about that world machine? It was trying to kill me." I offer up holding up my finger for emphasis.

"It was programmed against intruders. It was trying to take the whole squad out."

I pull at my upper lip, "yeah that's true enough. But what about those scorpion things! That was personal."

"Not personal, personnel. Only you and Dutch were on the mission as I recall your report Yaz. And they worked over Dutch more than you."

"You're not going to let me resign are you?" I ask glumly.

"Nope. Feel better having talked it out?" The Colonel asks me brightly.

"Not really, no." I answer and sit in a blue funk across the desk from her.

"Well, I'm glad we had a chance to have this little chat Yaz. Now can we get on with the commendation and promotion?"

I shake my head. They may not let me leave, but I can refuse a promotion. "I don't want to be a sergeant. The minute you get that extra stripe on me you'll ship me off to some newbie squad and make me exec. I don't want that."

"What if I give you the stripe and promise not to remove you from the Mohawk?"

"Too many chefs spitting in the soup. A squad needs one sergeant and I am with the best. There must be some eager beaver you can peddle a stripe to?"

Carla Hendrix leans back in her chair and gives me the once over, "I have a hundred Yaz and not one of them deserves it. Now you on the other hand do. So here is what I am going to do, I'm making you take the commendation. I think this is your fifth..."

"Sixth," I correct and the Colonel nods to me.

"Sixth, and I am also making you take the stripe..."

"You can't do that!" I protest cutting off an officer for the second time.

"Yes I can under extraordinary circumstances clause."

I grind my teeth, "yes you can do that."

"Finally I am guaranteeing you'll remain on Mohawk until you want your own command or Sean throws you off his ship. Congratulations Sergeant Aatiq!" And she reaches over shakes my hand and touches my sleeve with her magic rank wand and like that I go from man wanting to retire with a whole skin to man made more of a target by my increased rank. Military logic you've got to love it.

I get up a bit dazed and start to leave when what the Colonel said sinks in. "What extraordinary circumstances?"

"Sean has all the details, I believe he's waiting on you so he can address the squad. Dismissed Sergeant Aatiq."

"I want to be called Yaz..." I say petulantly.

"Dismissed Sergeant Yaz." I salute realizing that is the last order I'll ever give a colonel and leave to hunt up the Mohawk and her denizens.

II

Deep Space Australia was like all of her class, big, burly, and ugly as sin. The squarish buildings that made up the main above ground portion of the place had the look of all military bases, all function no imagination. The small E-class world on which it sat had no name just JZ-21-12. And that was about everything you needed know.

Colonel Jack G. Taylor had worked his whole career, no, his whole life to command a place like this. Now he was reduced to watching a gang of mutineers drag the mighty base toward destruction along with Jack Taylor's career. He peeked around the corner of the bridge only to get a shot that ricocheted off the stanchion he was hiding behind. "You son of a bitch Markus I'll kill you for that!" He shouts then snaps off a couple rounds in the general direction of what was once his first officer.

"Ha! You never could shoot straight Never Fail," his number one taunts. But Taylor shoots straight enough when Imamura his sensor expert tries to cross the bridge to a closer position. The shot catches the woman in the side blowing hole you could put a fist through and destroying the beautiful young woman in an instant.

"How's that for shooting Markie boy?" Two could play the taunting game. He wipes some of Imamura's brains and flesh off himself, turns and slithers on his belly to the emergency hatch set in floor. Maybe his Type-9 was set too high and could puncture the equipment, but so what? At this point Jack Taylor was fighting for what remained of his life. It was this or a court martial. Of course he'd rather kill Markus and regain control of the base and walk out with a whole skin, "ah if wishes where fishes Jackie boy, we'd all be kings." He whispers to himself as he wipes sweat off his forehead and lips. His mom used to say that. He never understood it but it seemed to fit.

III

I find Sarge waiting patiently for me next to the scaffold that cradles the Mohawk. How am I supposed to act to my superior when I hold the same rank as he does? I step up salute crisply, "reporting for duty Sir." I say in my best drill sergeant voice which is none too good. Then I glom onto his sleeve and start to giggle. "Of course! I should've guessed it couldn't be that easy." I shout out loud as I count the four stripes on my Sergeant's sleeve, then note I only got three.

Sean starts to laugh and pats my shoulder, "good to have you aboard Sarge."

I think that over, "can you still call me Corporal? I mean it just feels right."

"Someday you've got to let go of me, you're as good as I am Yaz, and a damn fine soldier." I just look at my boss, he twists his smile, "get aboard Corporal. We have people that need rescuin'."

We all gather around the bridge and Sarge stands arms clasped behind his back. The flicks a switch and holo pops up showing row after row of prefabricated Engineer Corp buildings. The base seems awfully big and worse dull. The grass plain it is set on seems to go on forever.

"That is grade A ugly." I say, and Dutch nods as she gives the holo her professional once over.

"This ladies and sergeants this is UES's newest base Deep Space Australia. Place should be open for business..."

"But..." Prompts Yeldon.

"Thank you for anticipating me, but the place has been dead quiet for the last fifteen or twenty days. Our mission is to rescue the crew."

"How are we supposed to cram that many people on the Mohawk? That place must hold a thousand people." Striker asks.

"True but the base is currently occupied by the Engineer Corp folks. They were supposed finish building the place, start up the telemeters and get ready for the base crew."

"Are ve sure they are still there, or alive?" Dutch asks beating me to the punch.

"I know the Corp commander, guy by the name Jack Taylor. His nickname is Never Fail Gail." Sean smiles realizing we don't get the joke, "his middle name is Gail. His second I don't know personally but he's an officer on the fast track. Name of Markus. Jack says he's nuts for Zane Grey.

"Who?" I ask trying to sort through all the names I know.

"Western writer from way back. Pretty good to, so I hear. So, tube up and get ready to jump to JZ-21-12." Sarge says and off we go.

IV

I crack an eye open as soon the needle pulls out of my big toe. "Someday I'm going to run out of toe." I say as I push the lid off me and look around. I count the noses , this time I am the only one awake. "Yeah! I get to do my job alone this time." I pad down to my quarters get dressed and head to the bridge. There I see HARVE's plates lit and I look at the E-type world. I shrug my shoulders, "you see anything that even looks dangerous?"

"I haven't but also I can't raise the base. Odd there is a power signature."

"So the generators are up, that's a start," I say trying to pierce the mystery by simply viewing the plate.

"I didn't say it was a generator. I have no idea what I am picking up but it is right in the middle of that base. Also, bits and pieces of the base have been destroyed. Single buildings or individual rooms. Everything that is important. I'm guessing one of those buildings is the radio shack."

"Gotcha. That, energy is familiar, I think." I answer distracted, "no space activity no ground activity. I'm waking the squad." I head down to medical and start the process. In an hour everyone is the bright and more or less their cheery selves. Sarge piles me, Yeldon, and Striker into a the penance with food and medical supplies and we head down to the planet. Yeldon and I are in full combat gear. It's not that we're looking for trouble we just don't want to be caught out by it. When we walk down the ramp and look around we see nothing worth reporting, that is until the firing starts. Yeldon snaps up her rifle and I push it back down. "We're friends! StarSoldiers!"

"The hell you say!" Someone somewhere screams back and takes another couple of pot shots at us. Good thing these are engineer types, they're lousy shots. Yeldon breaks left and I go right then slap the ramp which seals. The shuttle takes off flown by Striker out of harm's way while Yeldon and I work our way into the maze of cube form pourstone buildings. This is the worst kind of fighting, that golden bee-bee could be right around the next corner waiting for you. I follow a line of buildings find nothing worth shooting at and start down the next row when a figure jumps out and takes a crack at me. The light bolt bounces off my armor. I dodge around a corner. "Yeldon," I call into my microlink.

"Five by five." Yeldon snaps back, I can tell she's out of breath.

"Switch to overload, these are humans. I'm not sure they're our people but let's not make bodies until we have to." I click over to overload, a setting that paralyzes the central nervous system. Yeldon clacks her tongue at me showing her displeasure at my order but I can see from a red telltale in my helmet display that she has obeyed. We plunge deeper into the base receiving one sniper shot after another. Whatever these guys are using they're useless against armor. That does not mean someone out there doesn't have something heavier. As I watch the HUD Yeldon knocks down a couple bad guys, that evens the odds a bit. Those two will be in a coma for about twelve hours, than wake up with a very bad hangover. "I'm heading to Command Center. You clean up out here." I get a small purple light telling me she got the message. As I start that way I find deep large holes where presumably buildings used to be. Whatever made those holes could defeat our armor I'm guessing. I find myself about half way to command central when a volcano explodes just to my left taking out an entire wall about two hundred meters behind me. I look around wildly but see nothing. I roll right and crawl to a small dip in the dirt path between buildings. This part of the base is only half finished at best, belaying Sean's assertion about "Never Fail Gail." I look around with sensors but whatever took out that building isn't using a power source I can detect. That means finding it the old fashioned way, i.e. eyesight. And until I find that thing it's no use heading to command central only to have it blow up in my face. I start a careful search making sure everything is missed, like my head, hands, feet, torso, etc. hard as I try I can't find a single clue as to the weapon or whatever is. As I search I keep an eye on Yeldon who is using a standard search and destroy pattern. Suddenly below her feet the ground blooms bright red in my HUD, "Jess!" I yell but it's too late the ground explodes and I watch as the crater is formed with her in the middle of the hole.

I carefully work my way to the crater, at this point anyone who wanted to be combative is either asleep or hiding so I throw caution to the wind and make more or less a straight line to the new crater. The ground is still smoking when I get there. I use binocs and sensors and find Yeldon's pipper on my HUD. I opt for rocket assist and leap over the edge of the crater. Speed might be Yeldon's only saving grace. I must fall at least one hundred meters straight down before I find a shelf of rock. It's not the bottom of the crater but Jess might have landed here, at least her pipper says she's here. I touch down using the powerful motors in my feet and look around. I find a piece of Yeldon's armor. And with my lousy luck it's the bit with the pipper built into it. "Perfect."

There's nothing for it, I take another big leap and start to fall. "Striker, I've got a man down." I say as I fall. "I repeat man down, contact Sean tell Yeldon is missing presumed injured." All I get back is a strange whine on every channel of the microlink. "Okay, I'm on my own." I say as I keep falling passing the two hundred meter mark when my spot lights start picking up a bottom. When I land I look around but find no Yeldon. I do however find foot prints and drag marks. With nothing better to go on I start following the drag marks. I figure someone found Jess and is dragging her to safety. Or anyway, away from here. I follow through smooth nicely finished tunnels, the engineers did good work down here though I am at a loss as to know why here and not above. As I round a corner a small amount of rock and dust explodes at my feet and then a few pings on my chest tell me the snipers are at their old tricks again. This time I don't hold back, I draw out a flash grenade and strike its butt and toss it toward my would be attackers. It really doesn't matter where they are, unless they have the same eye protection I do they'll be blind in seconds. Sure enough the flash goes off and the tunnel becomes very peaceful. I move forward and find about ten people; I'm sure they're people by scanning their vital signs. Right now they're trying to get the spots out of their eyes and I take advantage of their condition to disarm the three that have small zip-guns. The things must have been worked up by them. The nasty little handguns could kill at close enough range against an unarmored target. Next I handcuff both their wrists and ankles so we can have a peaceful conversation. I let the shock wear off and sit down on a crate and point my Type-10 in their faces.

"Now how about you folks answer some questions for me." I start out. All of these people are underfed, dehydrated, dirty and most seem beyond exhaustion. "Does anyone here speak Universal?"

A man straightens his crude tunic, wipes his face by rubbing it on the tunic, it only makes him dirtier but I'm not going to mention the fact. "My name is Jack Taylor, Colonel Jack Taylor. United Earth Engineers Corp."

"And I'm the tooth fairy nice to meet you." I say. If this clown thinks I'm falling for that he's lost his marbles. Come to think about it, he probably has lost his marbles.

"I am Jack Taylor. These are my loyal officers and spacebees."

"If you're Jack Taylor, what's your nick name? And don't anybody say a word or you'll find out what a Type-10 can do to a human body. Not pretty."

He tries with as much dignity as you can muster in his condition and say quietly, "they call me Never Fail Gail. My middle name is Gail."

"What the hell are you doing like this Colonel? And what's the idea of attacking StarSoldiers? And one last, what the hell has happened to this base?"

"Over the last month members of the construction regiment mutinied and attacked the rest of us. We've been hiding out down here trying to get control back of the base."

"Okaaaayyy, have you seen another StarSoldier? She fell through the crater you tried to kill us with."

"We lost the battle with Markus for her. She is their captive. They'll try and strip her armor and weapons and use them." A disheveled member of his team says, it takes me a second to realize the pile of mud is a woman.

"Lost cause I'm afraid each suit is programmed to a specific set of genes. Now, I am going to release you people make your way to the surface. There try to contact Mohawk ask for Sergeant Murphy."

"Rolly-polly runs that boat!" Taylor ask and for the first time he shows an emotion other than exhaustion.

"Well, Sergeant Sean Murphy is CO." Taylor claps his hands and laughs. Seems we can't go anywhere in the universe without somebody knowing my boss. "I'd love to talk to Rolly but we have no communications. Everything was wrecked by Markus and his thugs, comm, food, water recycling, building machines. You name it they destroyed it if it was a machine."

"Okay take this," I and I hand the Colonel a small communicator. "I take it Markus is the one with the big cannon blowing holes everywhere?"

"No, no," the mound of rags shakes her head at me. I swear I see lice fall off as she does so. But it could just be dirt. "Every twenty three hours, fifteen minutes and forty five seconds there is an energy release. We have no idea what causes it."

"Good to know, that gives me some time. If Markus and his people are armed like you then I don't have too many worries. Get to the surface." Taylor gives me the skinny on where to find the mutineers and heads out with his folks topside. I turn back into the maze of tunnels and using Taylor's rough directions I soon find base camp of the mutineers. These two warring camps were less than kilometer apart. I move cautiously but make steady progress until I find two guards posted just in front of a couple of burning torches. I have to shake my head, they can't see and are silhouetted by the firelight. I'd pull another grenade but the entrance of their stronghold is too deep for me to get everyone inside. I fire taking the two guards down. Then I wait as some of the rest come running out. About five folks armed with zip-guns race out of the cave guns blazing. Okay well, popping small projectiles fly around the cave bouncing off walls, stalagmites, and me and achieve nothing. One by one a put people out and fight my way down the throat of the cave. When I reach the end one male, I can tell because his more or less nude stands over Yeldon his zip-gun pointed at her helmet.

"I'll do it!" He screams at me.

I'm about to say "go ahead," the helmet is as tough as the rest of the armor. But Yeldon finished the guy off with a boot into his family jewels. His face goes beat red, and he cries out and falls to the ground.

Yeldon is slow to get up but the suit helps her. When she's upright she walks over to me and tosses over her shoulder at the guy, "wave that thing somewhere else." She looks me up and down and says, "you took your time."

"Isn't there a reg about abusing a new Sergeant?"

"No there isn't now let's get." She says. I hold up my finger meaning one moment I plug into her suit. She's has a minor concussion from the fall and her left arm is broken. Her legs seem okay so I gesture for her to head upstairs and explain how. With Yeldon safe or at least safer I turn back to the group of prisoners but I quickly realize the five or six people I have in custody are not the whole group and Markus is not among them. The man is smarter than I gave him credit for. I poke around the cave and find many hidden exits from the main room and also from the side chambers that make up this cozy little hole in the wall. I lead my prisoners out and we make for the surface.

V

"You know Markus," the small man says as he stretches and looks back at the last hide out. "I'm really beginning to doubt your leadership."

"You know what Caruthers," Markus says his zip gun in hand pointed right at the other man's stomach, "I'm tired of your belly aching." And with that Markus fires the deadly little slug blowing a hole into Caruthers. At first the small man looks down at the remains of his destroyed belly, rolls his eyes up into his head and collapses. "Anybody else feel like expressing their discontent?" Markus says but what's left of his followers stay mute and simply do their best to put one foot in front of the other. The last attack by Taylor had destroyed their last food supplies. Markus looks over the next set of caves and speculates out loud, "how the hell did Taylor get an infantry suit? And get it to work?" Again nothing but silence greets his questions. Looking over his shoulder he asks, "nobody wants to venture an opinion?" Looking at the dirty, ragged, shambling mounds he once called soldiers he realizes their beyond opinions. "Fine, let move out. We need a place to sleep."

VI

Sean Murphy didn't recognize "Never Fail Gail" as he walked up to meet him in the med pit. His twenty or so people were laying around the small medical bay of Mohawk patiently waiting their turn with Striker. Sticking his hand out Taylor takes it limply and is barely able to stand the light pressure Sean uses for the shake. "Jack what happened?"

The man's eyes finally focus as if he seeing Sean Murphy for the first time, Sean could almost feel the penny dropping in Taylor's head as he recognized an old friend. His eyes grow feverish and haunted, "you have to kill Markus! Sean you have no idea what a Satan that devil is. He killed fifteen of my best people and then went on to wreck the base! I am giving you a direct order Sergeant Murphy, get your people down to the surface hunt down that rabid dog and kill him." It's as if that burst of hatred takes all the stuffing out of Taylor who slumps, his eyes again defocus, and he lapses into muttering. Sean just stands there looking at the wreck of a man wondering what could've happened down there when a light touch from Striker brings him back to the current problem.

"I've run brain scans on every one of these people. All of them are suffering from moderate to severe paranoia, coupled with dementia and dangerous psychosis. My guess is Sergeant another couple days on that planet exposed to whatever did this to them and they'd all be in a catatonic coma, after that death."

"Could Markus's people be in the same condition?" Sergeant Murphy asks but Doctor Striker is way ahead of him.

"I've checked the prisoners, their worse. And one other thing Sean," that perks up Sergeant Murphy's ears. Not because of the breach of protocol but because Marko never broke protocol, "I've run scans on Yaz and Yeldon. Both are showing the same signs. Not pronounced they weren't exposed long enough."

Stark terror hits Sergeant Murphy's heart, now his people were going crazy, "will they end up like that?"

"No, no, not at all Sergeant, in fact they're getting better. Probably because their natural mental defenses are kicking in." Striker says, "I've given them both some Valerian and put them to bed. Few hours sleep is what they need. "

"That's it then they can't go back down." Sergeant Murphy mumbles and Striker nods his ascent. "That leaves me and Dutch."

"And me," Striker offers.

Murphy shakes his head emphatically, "not a chance, I'll need you here to treat us when we get back. What can you do for Taylor's people?"

"I'm sedating them and giving them as much bed rest as I can. But they need psyche-ward level care. I can't do that here."

"Don't put Jack out yet, I want to talk to him."

Striker gives a wry smile, "Sergeant don't believe a word the man is telling you. His world right now is made up of hallucinations and trauma. He doesn't know what's real and what isn't. I'm truly sorry Sean, you're on your own." Striker turns back to his patients leaving Sean Murphy more at sea than when he started.

Heading down to the main bay Murphy finds Dutch prepping the shuttle full armor suit on. That was what he expected. Simple process of elimination made it inevitable that Dutch and he would be on the next trip planet side. What he is not expecting is Yaz in full gear with Yeldon in tow. "You two are staying here." He says and points them out of the bay.

"You can't search an entire planet with two people," Yeldon offers.

"Four isn't much of an improvement." Sergeant Murphy fires back. "Now based on what you two discovered, I have a pretty good idea where Markus and his band are."

"And between the four of us we can wipe them out," Sergeant Murphy's head snaps to look at Yaz. The same cherry smile that lights up Yaz's handsome face is there but the ease with which he talks about killing is way out of character. Looking the man over Sergeant Murphy realizes the worst part of mental illness is, it leaves no outward mark.

"You two are staying here. I want scans and brilliant ideas understood? I don't care how you get them just get them. I want you two, to figure out what that strange energy signature is that's blowing holes out of the planet. I want to know what happened to our people down there. And above all I want you to check in with Striker every four hours. You miss once, and you're cleaning induction tubes for a month."

Yaz and Yeldon give snappy if disappointed salutes and march out. All this time Dutch keeps humming and working on her ship. She turns and smiles, "Ve are ready Sarge."

VII

After Sarge's threat I head to Striker let him scan me he tells me to get some kip but I'm too angry for that. He relents and says I can work on the bridge until I get sleepy. He hands me two more Valerian which I down, I'm not sure why I am so angry right now. Striker says it'll pass, I hope he's right. But I can't quite shake the feeling that something must be done other than Sean's limp wristed approach to the mutineers. I wander up to the bridge and find Yeldon hard at work, "you couldn't sleep either huh?" She comments and I nod.

I sit down start looking over the scans that were made while Yeldon and I were on the surface. "HARVE is there anything more than what I am seeing?" I ask peeved that so little has been done.

"I'm sorry Yaz that's the best we could do in so short a time." HARVE answers.

"You're best ain't good enough HARVE. Not by a long…" I drop my insult to HARVE as I watch another hole explodes outward from the planet. This time I get some good data. "Yeldon, have you ever seen an energy pattern like this one before?"

"I can't say I have," Yeldon answers as she is engrossed in her readings. "Still no sign of the mutineers. I will continue to scan."

"Want to know something?" I ask.

"Not really Yaz, I am busy here," She says which is about what I expected.

"Jess listen to me and stop scanning that's an order." She sighs audibly and turns those gorgeous green eyes on me. If they were cobra's I'd be dead as a door nail right now. "No one in history has seen this energy pattern except in one place. Never."

"Okay," she says crossing her arms and keeps boring here green cobra's into my baby browns.

"Jess how do you feel right now?"

"Annoyed at the schmuck that's keeping me from working while asking me stupid questions, now make a point." I wait and hold her gaze. A blush hits her cheeks and she uncrosses her arms, "geez, Yaz I am sorry."

"Don't be, that energy pattern has been bothering me since we first saw it. Jess, that's the same pattern as a human brainwave. A disturbed human brainwave to boot. The planet, or more likely something on or in that planet is sending patterns of a human mind out. It's so powerful it's even reaching the ship, and it's altering our brain patterns to fit it." I lean back and close my eyes. "That's why those people become what they are, savages looking only to kill. There are no mutineers down there Yeldon never where." I open my eyes and look at Yeldon closely. "We've got to get back down there. Sean and Dutch are in trouble."

"Let's just bring them back." Yeldon offers.

"Comm is down. No way to talk to them. Even if we could I doubt Sarge would listen to us in our condition, what he doesn't realize is it's his condition as well. What he and probably Striker don't realize is their minds have been effected as well. They figure you have to be down there." I say.

"What about Striker?" Yeldon asks and I can see the force of my logic is starting to penetrate.

"Marko is effected too, we can't be sure his diagnosis is accurate based on his own mental state. But, and this trumps everything, he's all we got for medicine. So we'll do what we can down there and he will do what he can here."

Yeldon nods puts her small chin into her palm and thinks. Leaning over she throws a few switches and says causally, "the transponder is switched on the shuttle we can follow Sarge down. Okay, let's go. One thing first, what's digging holes?"

End

"I don't know, yet. But I am certain it is connected. Let's get going. HARVE?" I call out and in seconds HARVE answers. "I know you are on crew medical condition alerts. That means you have to report to Striker if we leave the ship."

"Yes I do Yaz. I'm sorry about this but it is standard protocol."

"Yeah, so report to Striker after we leave."

"As you are affected by alien technology Yaz I will have to ignore your order and report right away."

"Do as you please HARVE just remember if we get stopped Ditch and Sarge go the way of the people in the medical pit."

You can't hear HARVE thinking anymore than you can hear me or anyone else who isn't you thinking. But the quiet is eloquent, "I suppose if I were to report to Striker just as you lift off that would be within guidelines Yaz. After all you'd still be on the ship more or less. But how do I know what you are proposing is a sincere effort on behalf of Sergeant Murphy and Pilot Hilda Comargo-

Vandergriff?" It's weird to hear Dutch's real name but HARVE is being cautious right now.

I shrug, "you don't HARVE. And there is nothing I can do to prove my intentions until I am on the surface."

"You're asking me to do something beyond my programming, trust."

"Yep," I answer simply.

More eloquent silence and a grunt finally HARVE says, "it's your show Yaz."

We leave the bridge and head to the penance which is sitting in its cradle un-serviced. It takes us an hour to do what Dutch can do in fifteen minutes but we get the job done right and start out after Sarge and Dutch fast as we can. Dressing for full combat we spiral the penance down to the surface. The transponder leads us back to the original landing spot. Due to how long it took Yeldon and I to prep the penance when we get there we find about six people unconscious, more detritus from the machine that's re-shaping minds. These folks are half dead and in a coma. I can't worry about them right now, some in fact most might be beyond saving at this point. My sergeant and Dutch are not.

"Over here," Yeldon calls out and I head to where she's standing. A clear set of foot prints matching the boots of powersuits are visible. I go back to the people run a quick check with my handscan though I already know the result. Sean and Dutch didn't put these folks to sleep. This area may look like a battle, but the only battle is against something none of us can see. We follow the track back down underground this time taking the long way and remaining in one piece.

We reach the last curve which forces us against the wall of the passage. Our audio sensors pick up human voices. I don't think we need the fancy tech, whoever is talking is doing so at full volume. Yeldon and I press against the cave and start a slow half walk around the last bit of path hoping not to dislodge rocks and soil and giving away our position. I can tell by the timber of the voice that whoever is shouting is not Sarge or Dutch.

"And I'll tell you something else. He picks his toes! What kind of colonel picks his own toes? I ask you two." I'm so close I can hear the footfalls of the speaker as he paces. Yeldon unslings her rifle and charges it for overload. I slip past a ledge of rock and get a full view is the speaker pacing back and forth with his worshippers surrounding him waving a Type-10 like it's a pointer. Dutch and the Sarge are seated in the middle of the circle their Type 10's pointed at their now helmetless heads.

"Uh-oh" Yeldon sums up the situation neatly I must say. I look carefully and realize shooting is out, our people no matter how good we are will get shot at close range. I feel around my belt and realize I didn't replenish my grenades. Checking Yeldon she has a fragmentation but nothing else. Yeldon press against me and passes me to take a knee and start some very carefully aiming. "Overload can be dispersed if you're good." She whispers into my microlink.

"Lucky thing you're good." I answer back. I don't let her see that I am crossing my fingers as she lines up her first shot. I hold Yeldon's breath for her as she puts her finger on the trigger then squeezes gently. The overload fires out in a great bright circle that slams into everyone facing our position. Those with their backs toward us are given just enough time to turn around when Yeldon takes her second shot and puts them out along with Sarge and Dutch, but misses the speaker. He looks up smiles weakly saying "missed me!" And runs out of the cave away from us and his troops. "Some leader," I think as I watch him scoot away. I don't have a shot so he'll have to wait for now.

"Damn! I missed." Yeldon concedes.

"I'm not complaining. Now let's sort this mess out." Getting down to floor level we drag our people away from the pile of bodies and start cuffing the others hand and foot. This time not because they are under arrest but just so we can more easily control them. There is nothing we can do for Sarge and Dutch they'll just have to sleep it off like the rest of them. One by one we carry the sleepers back the penance. Once we get all twelve folks in, including Dutch and Sarge I wave Yeldon to take off. "I'll wait for the next bus." I say as I close up the penance and watch our pretty bird lift off. Once out of sight I get ready to explore when I feel rather than see or hear a shadow behind me.

"Just keep your hands where I can see them soldier boy." The voice says and I roll my eyes.

"Didn't that patter go out with 2-D entertainment?" I turn to see the speaker is stand right behind me a Type-10; by the looks of it Sarge's; in his hands pointed at my head. "Am I addressing Dmitri Markus?" I ask.

He nods his head way too much and makes clucking noises like a chicken. Anyway what I think a chicken sounds like. "Yepper, that's me pilgrim."

"Commander Markus listen to me."

He smiles holds up a single finger wags it at me and says, "Ah, ah, that's Long Sheriff Markus!"

This guys so out of it he doesn't even know who he is. This is going to take more than mere verbal gymnastics. "Whatever," I say annoyed.

"No if you are going to address the esteemed Markus you have to play fair!"

"Fine," I say through clenched teeth, "Long Sherriff Markus. You have been exposed to some kind of field or device on this planet that has destabilized your brainwaves. Please let me help you."

"What did you call me?"

"Long Sherriff, like you asked." I say reaching exasperation at a furious pace.

"No I mean before that," he says waving the rifle around again. People who treat weapons so carelessly make me nervous.

"Could you point that somewhere else at least for now?" I ask and he drops the snout, I've never noticed how ugly the Type-10 really is. Until now when a madman is waving one in my face. "I called you Commander Markus."

"That name rings a bell," he says and his eyes unfocus and I can almost see the conflict in his mind as he tries to grope back to reality. Suddenly his eyes lose all luster and intelligence and I can tell Commander Markus has lost the battle. At least for now. He whips up the rifle and snapping off a quick shot that plunges through my left thigh he runs away.

Looking down I see the blood starting to spread and I feel the suit's pressure gel seal the suit and my wound. I take a careful step and realize he only nicked the flesh. I am very lucky judging by the vegetation behind me that is melted and blasted. I take a few tentative steps and start to follow Markus. As I go I load a small metal sphere into the under-pump of my rifle and taking aim I fire. The tracking device lands on his back. He's so intent on getting away from the posse; i.e. me; he fails to notice, partner.

Walking is painful as all get out, but oddly I can run with little discomfort as Marko likes to call my pain when he's the one inflicting it. I chase the man until we reach yet another hole in the ground. He dives in head first, Allah protects the innocent and fools. I hope. As I reach the hole I feel a tremor and stark terror crashes into my heart almost as sharply as the shot I just took. Looking around I try to see something that indicates just where the hole is going to form but the entire horizon lifts as if a giant hand is pushing underneath a sheet of earth. At my handscan the chronometer tells me I have half an hour before another hole is blown out. I look down the hole Markus dived down and see him at the bottom holding the weapon steady on me. Sometimes I wish Allah would go find something useful to do, other than saving nut jobs.

He giggles like, well like a maniac and fires spraying the area around me as I lay flat on the ground. When the barrage is over I look down and Markus is nowhere to be seen. At least by my human eyes. I pull up the handscan and watch him race down a deep tunnel. He never pauses as he runs, which leads me to believe he has a definite place in mind. I rig up a line and repel down to the bottom and follow. The ground is uneven and I have to walk, feeling my wound every step of the way. "when I catch up to you...I'm going to rip out your heart Long Sherriff." I say out loud as another sharp pain jolts my body. Then I realize what is happening to my brain and I swallow back the rest of the curse. We wind and twist through one tunnel after another until Markus runs out of places to go. He enters a small gallery of stone and there takes up a fighting position waiting for me. I start to move toward the gallery when the signal suddenly stops. He's found the tracker. I see the broken remains of it go flying out the mouth of the gallery to strike the opposite wall making smaller pieces of the pieces. I look at my rifle and fight my desire to kill the mutineer and lock my weapon on overload. I seal up my suit and feel around my belt and realize I don't have any useful grenades unless I want to blow the guy to bits. Which I do, I really do. But that's not the mission. I'll have to trust my armor.

"I know you're out there bad guy. Come on! Take me on mano-a-mano. But I warn you I am fast." Okay Tex has just got to shut up. I pick up a rock and dodge just to the side of the cave mouth and toss it in like a grenade. It does the trick. Markus thinking he's going to be blown to bits rolls out of the cave spraying the outside with rifle fire all at waist level. I am laying flat. "Gotcha!" He shouts in triumph.

"Nope," I answer and plug him in the belly with one good shot that bowels him over and makes him drop to the ground asleep and disarmed.

"Good shot!" I hear behind me and turn to see Yeldon behind me waving a tracker at me.

"Shucks ma'am, twert-nothin." I say with as good a Texas draw and I can must and then I look down at Markus and at the gallery. Sitting in the middle of the place is a pearl. The size of three men the sphere looks like a shiny new pearl. I check my handscan but it doesn't make so much as a beep. "Are you getting anything from that, huh…thing?" I ask and Yeldon looks it over carefully scans it by holding her handscan next to, over, on, and under it. She gets nothing. I step over and decide the old fashioned approach might help. I reach a hand out and touch a solid surface. I can feel the pressure of my glove as I press on the side of the pearl. But according to my handscan, this pearl is not here.

"Okay how can something be here and not here at the same time?" Yeldon asks me as she shakes her handscan.

I shrug, "it just can." Okay sue me I'm not at my most scientific after being shot. I decide to go about this another way and start to scan the energy pattern. "Sure enough we are at ground zero Jess. In fact, if we stay much more than another hour down here the pearl will drive us mad. The amount of energy this thing must need to operate…Down!" I'm cut off from the rest of my summation when the ground shakes and the pearl glows bright red. A perfect ring of ruby red energy escapes from the equator of the pearl expanding until it contacts the walls of the gallery and starts to bounce around the place then races away is if it's a wild animal. Out the cave mouth it goes ricocheting off the walls, ceiling, floor and away from us. As we get back up

I see the searing marks on Yeldon's suit. And it takes considerable heat to do that. Yet I feel nothing as it past over me.

"That's the hole digger isn't it?" Yeldon asks but all I can do is nod as I try and catch my breath.

I pull it together and say, "let's get Commander Markus and leave."

Yeldon puts her rifle against his head and looks at me a smile I have never seen on her face before gives me cold chills. "We could just end it here, mutineer you know."

"Jess," I say as calmly as I can and hope she doesn't pull the trigger. She looks into my eyes fingers the trigger, removes it, puts her finger back on and nudges Markus with the rifle. I can see the internal conflict on her face. The true Jessica Yeldon wins after a few seconds and she puts her rifle away. "GAWDS Yaz let's get away from here."

"Let's go home Jess." I say and picking up Markus we start our way back up.

"How are we going to stop that, pearl thing?"

"We aren't Yeldon. We are going to leave this planet alone. One of two things will happen, the pearl will destroy the planet. It is the energy it's been releasing all this time that dug out these caves. Or two, it will die. In any event we don't have anything in our little arsenal of human tech to stop either."

Six Months Later

Jack Taylor looked out at the soft morning beach light and smiled. He was now convinced this was Finale and not another illusion set up by Markus.

Today was a big day for the Colonel. He straightens his cap pulling at his cuffs just a bit he opens the door to his room turns left and marches precisely ten steps, turns with parade ground precision and knocks twice and opens the adjacent door. Looking over he sees the figure in the dark. A shadowed arm turns on a small desk lamp with a restricted wave. The face is lit. Jack Taylor waits for the reaction. At first there is none. The man just stares at him passively. "How are you Dmitri?" He ask quietly. Waiting for the torrent of hate and bile to wash over him from this man.

"I'm fine Colonel. It's good to see you Jack. I'm sorry, I've been sick. I'd get up and salute if I could." Jack notices the restraints securing ankle and wrist to the bed frame.

He smiles gently, "I was hoping you and I could play a game of chess?"

"Not right now," Markus says and smiles. "But I'd like to hear Riders of the Purple Sage."

Jack Taylor laughs shakes his head. "You and your cowboys."

"It's not just cowboys, there are Indians too! Fair maidens to rescue." Markus says a smile a meter wide on his face.

Sitting down Colonel Jack Taylor pats his second on the foot. Opening the well worn reader he clears his throat. "A sharp clip-clop of iron shod hoofs deadened and died away, and clouds of yellow dust drifted from under the cottonwood…What is a cottonwood?"

Markus smiles, "A type of tree silly."

"Should I go on?" Jack asks politely.

"Please do. Thanks Jack. You're the best friend a man could have." Markus says and closes his eyes ready for the rest of the tale.

"You too Dmitri, you to."

Feedback

Beta Readers

Email

rc.coyne@yahoo.com

Looking forward to hearing from you! Please email your desire to be a beta reader.

Who I am

I love telling stories and the more out of this world the better. I hope you enjoy my musings as much as I enjoy spinning them. I spend my time writing, running my business, riding my bike too fast everywhere and catering to my cat Ares! Oh, and writing.

COPYRIGHT

© copyright C. R. Coyne 2024

Copyright © 2024 Although the author and publisher have made every effort to ensure that the information in this book was correct at press time, the author and publisher do not assume and hereby disclaim any liability to any party for any loss, damage, or disruption caused by errors or omissions, whether such errors or omissions result from negligence, accident, or any other cause. This item is a licensed product. However, I do not claim ownership of non-C.R. Coyne images used in designs. Copyrights and/or trademarks of any character and/or image used belong to their respective owners and are not being sold.

World Machine

"From the heavens the stars fought their courses, they fought against Sisera..."

Judges 5.20

A StarSoldier Chronicle

Raven Coyne

My feet are so far off the ground that I have to look down to see where I'm landing. My feet almost kick in midair as I find myself coming back down with positive mass to the deck plates. There's nothing wrong with the gravity unit, far from it. If it were broken I wouldn't bother to look down, because I'd never get there. As I land I give a hearty OOF! And then sprint up the passageway and slide onto the bridge to be greeted by a sour look from Sergeant Murphy for my lack of military decorum. I take my seat like a bad schoolboy and start to ignite my panels to life and see the empty void that is space spread out before me. If the ship weren't rocking back and forth I'd yawn at the view. But it's the very normalcy that is so frightening, whatever is swatting this ship around like a dog's chew toy is so far invisible, or so far away it might as well be.

Clearing his throat after a minute or two Sarge asks me, "see anything worth reporting?"

I glare so hard at my plates I'm afraid I'll need reconstructive surgery on my corneas. I shake my head and mumble, "not a thing. Just that gas giant we've been looking at for a week off and on." Then I start looking at my other readout only to get interrupted by Sarge clearing his throat, I look up and see Sarge standing patiently until I say, "nothing to report, sir. Still scanning." Then I go back to glaring. Sean finally drops the drill Sergeant act and comes over to look at my plates and instruments. "Answer me this, could any phenomena in real space effect this ship while in Overdrive?"

I shake my head and look up at my boss, "nothing can, for those few seconds, we are no longer here. You can't effect something that does not occupy normal space. It's like this, we on occasion pass right through the event horizon of an inconveniently placed black hole. But we're never crushed or whatever happens to you when you fall into a black hole. Why? Because our mass is not occupying the same dimension as the hole."

"Okay I understand that much, but we were crossing this area in Overdrive and the ship got yanked out of wherever it was and deposited here.

And whatever that...ah, whatever it is, it's now dragging us toward it even on reactive drives."

I nod and Sarge pulls on his lip then scratches his faux beard a few times and shakes his head. "And there is nothing out there to look at."

"Well, there is," I offer trying to put this symposium on a scientific basis, "just not in the wavelengths our eyes can see in." I throw a few switches and point to my gravity display which shows an ugly bulge growing bigger as we keep barreling through space out of control. Sarge nods and flips a few of my control panels and there in the middle of my plate is a glowing mass, glowing in this case in X-ray. "Now what is that I wonder?" I say and start running as many scans as I can and trying to sort facts in my head as fast as I can. As the answers pop out of my console I whistle and look up at Sergeant, "it's a sun, a star that is moving at one-quarter the speed of light and is heading right at us. Dutch let go for a minute, I'll drive."

"Must you?" Dutch asks miffed at the idea of losing control of the ship. After all, she is the pilot. But I'm the superior rank. I nod and she slaps the override button and I start some not-so-fancy maneuvers. "See what's happening?" I say to Sarge "Every way I go the star keeps crawling back into my plate right dead ahead." Sarge looks at me sharply, I'm already over my lack of military decorum leeway now, so I say quickly "Maybe I shouldn't say dead."

"Maybe you shouldn't, but that does seem to be the end result of this little side trip. Are you telling me that things is maneuvering to counter us?"

I would have said yes had the Mohawk not decided to spin uncontrollably. Sending all of us from ceiling to floor to each wall with every revolution. Somehow Dutch drags herself to the pilot's chair straps in and starts to move the stick getting no response, she looks at Sarge who yells, "override!" She gives a weak smile pushes override off and starts to fight the ship. I don't really notice any change as I again get slammed from ceiling to deck plates. "And here I was hoping for more ace pilot!"

I grumble then fight my way to Dutch's station by crawling across the ceiling waiting for the roll and fall right next to her. It's not the best way, nor the least painful way of getting here but at least I'm here. I start to work the stabilizers while Dutch dives us through the spins and I apply rear and counter thrust. The Mohawk finally decides it's had enough and starts to flatten out offering Dutch the chance to regain control. Once we're level she looks at me those big beautiful eyes glittering "Zee! No perspiration!"

I roll my tongue around my mouth and say, "I think you mean no sweat. And thanks Dutch you are the best."

She nods and smiles and gives me a shooing motion with her free hand, "you do...ahhh whatever it is you do and I'll fly. Now go avay."

"Nothing like gratitude for ya," I head back to my station and start to run more scans trying to figure out this beast that's tossing us around. I finally decide to try a long ball play and look for mechanical readings from the star and for the first time, my guess is right. I find myself leaning back and just looking at my plates. Sarge must notice my reaction we walks over and looks over my shoulder.

"That thing is mechanical?" He says incredulous and starts shaking his head no. I want to agree with him but the facts are staring me right in the face so I do the only thing possible, I shrug my shoulders. "Okay, how do we get away from this windup toy?" Sarge is great at getting to the point.

"Ve don't," Dutch pipes up from her station. I watch her eyes, she's concentrating on the monster and trying to avoid getting us fried. "I've done everything I know. It won't let us go."

I look over at Sarge, "she's right, we don't get away this time." Sean looks down at me with a desperate look then grips my console.

"Dutch full ahead, get us in orbit then prepare to land."

Striker, and Yeldon who up until now have stayed silent as their jobs don't include flying or assesses space phenomena start to talk at once. Striker with that big deep voice of his wins and says "That thing is over two million degrees. There is no landing on it, just burning up in it."

Yeldon nods saying "can't we orbit until we figure something else out."

This is where I pull rank again, "Dutch take us in." She begins to question me but I'm in no mood, "now!" She punches the buttons savagely and takes the stick and I add, "it'll be alright." Dutch starts to guide the ship into land. She circles the strange flaming globe once, it is much too small to be a sun, the closer we get the better my readings get therefore I find a nice shady patch and order Dutch to park the bus. Mohawk bucks a few times pushing her nose up and fussing over the turbulence of the hot gasses we're passing through then suddenly the ship smoothes out. I look over at Dutch, "told ya."

Not impressed she says "sure." And lands.

Striker keeps looking at his bio readouts and realizes after a moment we're not dead and giggles. Yeldon sensible as always pulls the metal blind down from one of the port holes and takes a look outside. For a second I think she is terrified by what she sees, but she just stands there unmoving. She finally whispers slowly, "Sarge you better take a look at this you'll never believe me."

Sean chuckles a little, "bet I will." And heads over and looks out acting as if he knew all along. And for all I know he did. I focus the cameras outside and we all get to look at the cool mountain glen we've landed in. The pine forest is beautiful and the lazy stream just north of the ship is a nice touch.

Striker top flight medico he is says, "well we won't cook to death."

"That's nice," I say and run a few checks trying my best to believe or at least trust either my eyes or my sensors. "Gravity is exactly one g, which is impossible. This star sports an oxygen, nitrogen atmosphere, which is impossible. And it's a lovely twenty-two degrees Celsius out there. Which again, as if you didn't need me to, but I must say it is impossible."

"How can a star double as an E-type planet?" Yeldon looks even closer at the main plate then asks the crucial question on everyone's mind, "could it be an illusion?"

Sarge looks over at me raising his eyebrows, "Yaz?"

"An illusion would suggest someone is controlling or at least manipulating our minds. Now that is possible. The soothe-lizards of Ralincon VI can do that to you. You see your heart's desire, instead of the ugly brute about to eat your head. But if you have a hand scanner the scanner would scream at you, it's a lizard about to eat your head. What I mean is we might be fooled HARVE cannot be."

Sarge punches the AI link allowing HARVE to interact with the biologicals on board. "HARVE what do you see out there?"

With dry whit HARVE answers, "Black Butte California." Sarge frowns and then nods. HARVE realizing that might have come out a little glib stays silent.

"Vhen do ve get to go outside und play?" Dutch asks throwing the anti-gravity spot on which allows the ship to hover in one place. Kind of like a ship's anchor.

"No one is going anywhere until we have just a few more facts..." Sarge says crushing everyone's hopes for being first out the airlock but the man's right this is too weird to allow anyone outside yet. Too bad though, it's a nice day. However, someone has to go outside and assess the damage to the ship from all that tossing around. So I get up and start to leave the bridge when I hear Sarge behind me, "where are you going?"

"Outside, to assess the damage," I say as if this is the most obvious thing in the world. Which it is.

"Not this time, I brought us here." Sergeant Murphy can be a most complex man when he wants to be.

I let slip, "you just want to be first out on a nice spring day." Sarge gives me a look I've rarely seen, "or not." I say quickly then add, "you are in command, however and not in a position to take first risks."

"In fact, that is exactly why I have to go out corporal. I want all of you watching me and with your other eye glued to your plates getting as much info on this place as you can. We might be here a long, long time."

"No hope of rescue sir?" Striker asks then blushes adding, "right no one is going to be looking for us on the surface of a rogue star."

Milton Keynes UK
Ingram Content Group UK Ltd.
UKHW020056181024
449757UK00011B/645